LUCY - THE TRUE GRIMOIRE

Birch and Kane Mystery
Detective Prequel

Kev Freeman

CONTENTS

1. SPARK

The flash hit me like a splinter, igniting a shock with enough energy to dissolve my embryonic thought of escape. In half a second, my priority turned from planning my redemption to the simpler, more achievable possibility of avoiding a simple refraction of light. How easy it was to compare the value of my life to a singular, fleeting brightness, but in this moment, one is quicker to resolve.

A reflex straightened my arms, raising my backside off the seat, which spun a quarter turn counterclockwise on its hydraulic lift. My elbows punched and locked with a click; over-extending the joints further than their full degree. I cast a sideways glance to my right, returning my attention towards the shimmering light, and attempted to locate the source of the flash.

I peered through my shop window, for a moment forgetting the reason as I considered the grime coated glass. It was overdue a clean, two months overdue. As the outside world came into focus, I traced the jagged line of rooftops which formed an uneven horizon beyond the dirt encrusted pane. The foreground took a breath, a gentle wind rippled through a tangle of loose branches, hurling fragile wisps of dormant twigs against each other, then nature exhaled. The breeze pushed clouds hurrying along an invisible conveyer belt of sky. In the distance, the tip of the closest of the twin crucifix of St. Joseph's church appeared and sliced into the evening air. There it was, the culprit, splitting and throwing shards of setting sunlight in random directions, like a flashlight held in the hand of a rabid monk.

Avoiding any thought about what lay in store, I became transfixed, almost hypnotized, by this spectacle. I couldn't dare to divert my stare. With no effort, I caught another golden ricochet. Bam, like a lightsaber, the glare blinded me for a moment as it scraped and stung at the backs of both eyes. I blinked, a delayed and fruitless effort to reduce the impact of the dazzle.

I dropped back into my chair. The hydraulic spring bounced as it absorbed the movement. My hands, now free to press their palms into my face, attempted to squeeze out the irritation from my eyeballs. As my eyes squished, flashes and circles of green swirled against the darkness of my blackened vision. Still disoriented, I forced my eyelids open and, through the swimming watery glare, refocused on the ornament fixed above a copper dome. The roof, an oxidized green metal, weathered through age. The crucifix, an advertisement, the instrument marking a greater story. I imagine its once sharp point stroking and etching upon the surface of the ether like a dot matrix printhead. The corroded bronze directing light and energy and authoring the swirling autumn sky above.

The twin domes of St. Joseph's provided support for the symbols of good, as they have done for over one-hundred and fifty years, and here I was preparing to issue marks of evil. Seen by all, the crucifix poked above the lichen laden slate roofs of the neighboring buildings. Reaching through the distorted twigs of oak trees and connecting through their twisted trunks to the earth below. These signs call out to their congregation, but today, as workers run about their last business, few realize the message or bathe in its power. I'm aware, but unable to resist or change direction. A retreat into the turmoil of my internal world is the only option.

"Rescind and return to the work of the pen."

The mumble fills the shop like the call of a beached whale. I still and listen for a moment. Then a gurgled riposte.

"Stick to your purpose, and I will stick to mine."

It's only now I realize it's my voice which fills the

shop; it echoes and waits for companionship. But there's nothing but the ticking of the clock, each click measuring her approach. A shivering chill runs down my spine. I know she is near, and I'm unable to prevent her arrival.

I'm trapped within one of these periods of mindless drifting into subconscious thought; their frequency becoming greater, the times when I'm paused behind the curtain of reality. Underneath my stiff body, the chair, a comfort for many, but not for me. The seat is hard and unfriendly. I must move against this spell, so I stretch.

I stretch further, hands raised towards the ceiling in a symbolic surrender, I suppose. A concert of cracking joints erupts as my spine arches and pushes the rear of my head deep into the surface of my custom-built Ronin client chair. The padding gives as the circular hole within the headrest with little resistance, and I push more to embed further, until my ears bend forwards with the pressure of the material behind. Constructed to offer a soft relaxation for my clients, whether they are face up or down, the chair is my business, the reason I bought it. Now, at last and with some relief, I experience the chair's cloud like embrace for the first time.

My fear subsides as a comforting warmth engulfs and swells around me as repayment. I try to relax, willing the chair to do its work. There's no option but to give in to the present and to the story it carries. Then, as I'm lowering my arms in submission, I hear my mother's voice echoing from my past. "Take deep breaths Greg." Her voice calming me when I got myself into a mess, which was more often than not. This time there is no-one to steady my thoughts, no-one to provide the reassurance I need. My breaths pull deeper and deeper, waiting for the calm. It will not show itself, however hard I try.

Outside, the sun has fallen below the point where it can challenge the crucifix; the sky turning a dark purple as the evening pushes away the remnants of day and the reach of the spidery branches tearing at its skirts. Now restored, my gaze moves from the fading glint of the church appendage and lower, towards a stream of people grazing the pavement. Their steps marked time, passing by without a sideways glance. The blue light of their glowing phone screens interspersed by the turn of bright neon shop signs hanging above. Solemn, gaunt faces illuminate without thought.

Behind me, the headrest creaks as I lean even further into the faux leather hole in its center. I pull forward. The release replays the sound in reverse as the padding expands and pushes the cushion to return to its resting place. For a second all around is quiet, until the void fills with the rasping fullness of my breathing. The vibration bounces from wall to wall, trapped within the confines of my workspace.

In my chest an amen break, hip-hop stutter of a beat bursts at my ribs. My right-hand crawls across my chest, measuring the rhythm of my heart as it pounds, marking time against the slow, steady tick of the long red finger of the wall clock as it circles towards the end. Outside, the LED streetlights burn the outlines of silhouetted tired stragglers into blurred motion, their shadows combine with those thrown by street trees onto a damp carpet of pavement. An anonymous herd, the figures hurry toward the warmth of their homes. For me, it's almost the hour to make ready my business.

2. TIME

Who am I? A simple, wide-eyed writer, story-listener, among a world of storytellers. I'm the one who anchors wispy, ethereal threads of human emotion to a foundation. Threads of anguish, happiness, friendship, distress, and sometimes, yes, sometimes, even hope. I record them, trapping and holding them close for the life of the teller. With little effort, I connect each personal story to the outside world. I retell these stories, not by the spoken or written word, but by their image. A tattooist: I embed emotions as colors and designs onto the body that carries them.

My name is Greg Bentley, 'Bomber' as I'm known to my regulars and to a few who may recount a younger me; and no, my tag has nothing to do with explosives, but relates to my previous life as a graffiti artist. I may tell more of that later. Right now, my priority is to relay the account which you're about to read. It is true, although your belief may depart long before absorbing this entire record. A fantasy of my mind? I will hold hope that you'll travel with me to the end, for the end is the reason I'm documenting this troubling event. Then, only after you have read the whole, will I accept your decision whether the events of the last four months happened as described, and whether you accept that 'she' exists.

For eight weeks I have marked time. Two dark months, more or less, with no resistance. The days filled by the cold and damp air, which covers London like a skin between November and February. I waited, following the directions as instructed. I remained alone, confined to my shop and its apartment. I observed seconds pass like grains of sand falling through an hourglass. The hands of my large white wall clock tick-toked forward. The story always moves onwards, round and around, towards the last appointment.

Going over the happenings, I closed my eyes and visualized again the manifestation of my story. My mind slowed, wandered, looping back to torment itself with the only questions it can hang onto. Why was I chosen for this? Why me? I suppose I can find answers, my answers, but are they the reasons for others? My ability to listen to people? My artistic skill? A promise made? Like a mother bird regurgitating food, I reviewed my life countless times. The events played in sequence, over and over.

Without warning, it found me. I attempt to uncover a lost memory. Something, anything, which should have alerted of this darkness. In the end, she found me. But I never hid. Not from her, anyway.

3. WORLD

Today is November 26th, but, for now, consider the date, the date alone. It's been ten years since the event that led to me being here. The moment that led to me being allowed to choose. It wasn't a happy day; the day marked by my grandad's death. It wasn't good that he died. He wasn't a wicked man. He was my hero. But I benefited from it, because his death precipitated his collection of old comic books being passed into my care. I was ten then, and those comics were the only things which could keep my attention for any period. Books and words without pictures did little to get through to my developing mind. They were nothing more than dancing, detached scribble.

Being an introvert with limited vocabulary and knowledge of grammar, I now rely on spell check to spot the most obvious errors in my writing. I didn't connect with school or learning at all. I needed something to build my world, to create my story. The Avengers, The Hulk, Spiderman, and Flash Gordon changed it all, twice.

My family visited grandad's place until I was about nine. His cottage was located somewhere in the countryside north of London, in Essex. I remember the drive out of the built up grey urban tightness of the city dissolving into a blur of green countryside, filled with trees and fields of rye and corn. Towns, villages, then hamlets in ever decreasing density until the countryside became everything.

Grandad's house sat alone at the edge of a small village. I recall a small corner shop, where you could get all the chocolate and soda a kid could need, marked our arrival. The store sat at one corner of a three-way junction, off which a narrow road led to the cottage; a red brick detached building with a huge backyard filled with flowers and herbs, and a greenhouse always at capacity with ready to eat tomatoes falling off their vines and just willing you to relieve them from their stems. The limit of the property, marked by an old wooden fence much taller than I, promised adventure beyond its bounds. It didn't disappoint. In the garden's corner, behind a large oak tree, an unlocked narrow gate led to a path. Pushing against the failing rusting hinges always elicited a grinding yelp as it opened onto an overgrown path.

I soon found, after some effort in clearing a way through, the path connected to a disused train track and then, about a quarter of a mile further, to an abandoned railway station. Free to explore, I played alone there for hours, climbing trees, drawing, laying on my back, staring up at the sky without ceiling and listening to life. Everything I do now if I get the opportunity, apart from climbing trees. I had no fear of heights, I still don't.

Hanging out at the house where my father had grown up felt good. It held a lot of memories for them both. On the top floor, in the spare bedroom, grandad kept what remained of his childhood and youth. The stuff moved there when grandma had died. Beside a mahogany wardrobe sat an old tea chest, a rough wooden crate with 'Ceylon Tea' printed at an angle on its side. Worn thin the letters held their stenciled form enough to still be legible. Rusty metal protectors ran down each corner and added to its junk-like appearance. Its lid was tight, squeezed against a metal lip, leaving only a small gap between the two. The first time I ventured to open the box, it took some effort because it looked like grandad had packed it some time ago. My first try at levering the top away failed. I couldn't get my fingers into the miniscule gap and almost lost a couple of fingernails trying.

After a hurried search through a draw full of jumble, I found an old screwdriver. I suspected it was grandads from his time working as an electrician. The worn handle was hard to grip, but the shaft and blade were free from rust and provided a good lever. Inserting its tip around and into the gap, I twisted the point back and forth until the join widened and the lid popped as it released its grip. I pushed my face into the dark of the gaping hole. Pursing my lips, I took a deep breath. The stale air filled my nose. I became addicted to the first smell of old paper and print ink.

Inside the container revealed contents which weren't 'Ceylon Tea', as it advertised. I brushed my fingers over the cover of a bright, cartoon styled magazine. As my eyes adjusted to the dark, I saw, piled deep, a treasure trove of comic books, layer upon layer, all waiting to be rediscovered. For now, I only needed one.

I grabbed at the first comic and out it came. On its cover, a blond man wrestled with alien creatures and called out for my attention. I didn't know if grandad would be alright in allowing me to be messing in his box. After all, I hadn't asked for his permission. Not wanting to risk having to put the comic back in its place, I got it out of the house. The old railway station would offer a shelter where I could relax and spend some time absorbing its content.

Using both hands, I flattened the comic and wrapped it around my front, pulling my tee-shirt to seal any gap. I ran down the stairs, hoping that no-one would notice my strange robotic posture and burst into the rear yard. Dad and Grandad were both busy in the greenhouse and I snuck by and opened the gate at the end of the garden. A customary metallic squeal of the hinges alerted them to my departure. Both men turned to stare in my direction.

Rotating halfway out of the opening, with my back against the gate post, I gave them both a quick wave and held my breath, anticipating discovery. To my relief, without hesitation, they both returned my gesture. Dad held up his wrist and tapped at it with his right index finger. "One hour Greg." He shouted. I nodded and closed the gate after me, its latch clinking into its holder. I took a deep intake of country air as it blew into my face.

Following the path, I made good time and arrived with relief at its terminus. Standing amongst a shroud of overgrown foliage, the derelict railway station. I took my place. Sitting with a thump, I landed on the empty platform with my back against the cold brick of the abandoned ticket office. I checked to see if I had any company. The building and the surrounding area had few visitors. Other than one dog walker, I don't recall seeing anyone else. I took the comic book from my pocket and laid on the ground. After smoothing the paper with the backs of both hands, I got it to lie against the platform, almost. I studied the cover for a while, then entered the world it contained.

The pages turned in a blur and the hour dissolved into a different dimension. Time ran away in the company of my imagination. An hour passed, and

I was late. I hurried back to Grandad's house, squeezed past the yelp of the gate, and scurried up the stairs and returned my loot to its regular place.

On my later visits, I would rush for the chest soon after my arrival. I would dig out a comic book at random, an episode of The Fantastic Four, Spiderman, Avengers, or my favorite, Flash Gordon. I would scamper away to my reading spot at the disused railway station to be engrossed by the ability of the artist to tell the story through small comic strip drawings and speech bubbles. While my friends took an interest in video game consoles, I consumed stories of superheroes and their adventures. I grew up reading these stories, but in reality, I was listening to my inner narrator describe my imagination. That voice became skilled at taking me to other worlds with unknown cities with strange names. I wasn't a reader; I was a listener.

One time, closer to the day my grandad became ill, I ran to my usual reading spot, Flash Gordon in hand. As I approached the platform, something had changed. Others had been there. The last time I had visited the brick walls was unmarked. Now the station is covered with painted signs and words. Most of the colored swirls were nothing more than scribbled nicknames, Joker, Crumb, and Spear. Other shapes formed intricate symbols. All lined with precise and super neat edging. The symbols had little meaning until now. Recent events and my own actions have enlightened my understanding. I remember something as I'm recalling the images. The thought bounces like a dream on waking, then disappears before I can touch it.

4. COMIC

Three years ago, after thirty years in the local planning department, my dad retired and implemented his, and my mum's, dream of moving to the south coast. Placed on the market, our house sold without delay; we had to move. I was not going with them. To be trapped in Southend, a community designed for those who had their own box full of stories, and with no disrespect to my parents, panicked me. I imagined being buried alive in a tub of jelly. Instead, I needed to figure out a way of making my dream materialize. A small studio where I could run a tattooist shop.

My salvation, the second that my grandad had authored, appeared as we prepared to move out to a new life. Tasked with clearing out the cellar, I stepped down the stone staircase into the cold, dark void. I hadn't been in a while. The last time to help my father deposit the tea chest after grandad's death. The box remained closed. I had had no urge to open it until now. It was alone and covered in dust from years of neglect. It was the first occasion I had tried to remove the lid since its move. Now, with stronger hands, the seal popped with a dull scrape.

I lifted the lid clear, bent at the waist and dropped my face into the opening, taking a deep breath. Trapped since they loaded it from grandad's house, the air released. I drew in the air, like the aroma of a wonderful wine. A familiar smell of publishing and ink filled me with nostalgia, took me back to its origin.

The contents revealed themselves differently than I recalled, in the main because I had grown more than a foot and a half in the time between openings. I reached inside the box with both hands, my fingers picked at the cover of the first comic they met like a fairground claw. The paper stuck, and I lifted it clear of its companions. It was then I caught sight of the illustration, a flag from my past. It was Flash Gordon.

I had studied this cover and its pages and incumbent drawings many times during my visits to the cottage, carrying them off to my private world at the railway station. I shivered when I realized I didn't remember the name of the village where my grandad's place was located; but I remembered this comic. I remembered it in some detail. It sat in my hands like it did those years ago. I placed the comic beside the tea chest and peered into the void.

Taller, I now had a different perspective of the inside

of the box and its contents. Beneath the surface of well-thumbed comics were stacks of other editions. With excitement, my fingers slid deeper. Avengers #78, Avengers #77, Avengers #76, Avengers #75. Hang-on, a descending order. Maybe at the bottom were first editions. The Avengers #1 perhaps. Could those be worth anything, something?

Leaving the box and its contents, I ran upstairs to my laptop. The search engine loaded, and I entered 'comic book dealers in London' I got in touch with a dealer who bought collections. Mr. Darington, he had a store in town, a short bus ride. The shop nestled close to Berwick Street Market. As I entered, I caught the familiar smell of paper and print, and it hit me, taking me to that moment, leaning into an old tea chest in granddad's cottage. Distracted, I stopped in my tracks and only came back to animation when an older man called to me from the rear of the store.

"Is it Greg?"

"Yes, Mr. Darington?"

"Yes, it's very good to meet you, Greg. Come on into the back."

Beckoning with a curled finger, he turned and disappeared into a doorway beyond the main retail area with its row upon row of classic comics guarding my path. I followed and joined him in his office. A small, dim room, lit by one desk light. Darington sat, shoulders hunched behind the dark oak table.

"So, what have you got then?"

"A few comic books, a collection, I suppose you would call it."

"Well, that's what I was hoping, eh?"

I pulled out the plastic folder from my backpack and laid out a small stack of my booty. A copy of Avengers #1 sat on top.

"There you go. I think I have about one hundred and twenty in good condition." I said.

Darington flinched, stretching forward from his slump before standing upright against the desk. His palms thumped either side of the transparent plastic envelope and he bent forward. His hands grabbed each packet, spinning them back and forth over the polished oak like a game of 'spot the queen'. Only we could both spot the queen today.

He looked at me and blew out his cheeks before sitting with care back in his chair. A creak emanated from him or his seat, difficult to tell from the stiffness that had gripped his frame.

"Well, these are special."

"Are you saying they're worth something?"

"Oh Yes, they are, indeed they are, especially that one." He placed his right hand on the desk and extended the index finger to point at the corner of Avengers #1.

"Look, I'm going to be straight with you. I'll make you an offer. No bullshit, it will be the best. You can take these away and ask other dealers, but they won't match it."

"How much?"

"How many comics do you have, you say?"

"I have the entire list here." I reached into my jacket pocket and pulled out the detailed list I had made before setting out. Under each title, Avengers, Superman and the others, a column of issue numbers, all beginning with #1, and most ending in the fifties.

He took it and resumed his stiff slump. His eyes scanned down the list and stopped at various points, leaving a pencil mark, and hurling a quick glance at me each time he did so.

"Well. You could get you a tidy sum for these if we auction off the best." Darington removed a large screen calculator from the top drawer of his desk and punched in the figures.

"Two hundred." He said.

"Two hundred. Hey, that's not too bad. It'll more than pay for my tube fare down here."

Darington laughed. I didn't think it was that funny. It was a fact, the fare was less than a tenner.

"If you want to walk away with a bank transfer, I can give you two hundred with no quibbling if you the rest and they are similar condition. You won't need to wait for an auction to get your cash. If you go elsewhere, you'll get offered thirty percent of my number and have to wait for the payout, guaranteed."

Darington scraped his fingernail down the list.

"Two hundred sounds good." I said.

"Yes, two hundred thousand, no quibbling. We have a deal?"

Two hundred thousand, he said. Two hundred thousand.

5. NORMAL

I used the money for a down payment for my shop with its apartment above. So, I now live just around the corner from where I grew up. My premises are in the middle of a row of various stores on Highgate Hill, bookended by Boyles & Co. on one end and a just renovated coffee shop, the Brewing Cup, on the other. A sushi restaurant, pizzeria, café, and general store make up the commercial offerings. Nothing much of note. The row of shops offers a range of services and goods for both the living and dead, all part of a thriving local business community in a large city.

The apartment is compact, but plenty big enough for more than one, maybe six at a push, I suppose, although I've never tested the space to that limit. Next to my bedroom is the bathroom. Both take up the space of the attic conversion on the fourth floor. The level below contains the lounge-kitchen area, and below that are a couple of spare rooms and another bathroom. I could lease out the two spare rooms if needed, but I like the quiet of my company, so I've not considered it.

The top-floor bedroom faces east, so, depending on the time of year, I get a good wake-up call when the morning sun hits the window. In winter months, the time of the call gets later. My faithful digital alarm does the job.

I sometimes peer out onto the backyards of the terrace homes in the rear of my home and onto lines of drying, washing, or kids playing. If I press my left cheek to the cold glass of the window and pop my eye as close to the surface as possible, I can observe the rear of Boyles & Co. the funeral directors. A paved yard where the 'clients' of such business arrive. Discrete black vans decant their passengers, then depart a few days later. A polished box, laid out in the back of a hearse, sometimes covered with flowers arranged in messages, celebrating a display of grief, 'MUM', 'DAD', or 'NANA'.

In front, the businesses lined the street. The brick buildings have stone decorative lintels and other features. The height of most of them has gone from three to four stories. I knew the street from spending all my life growing up in its shadow. All my boyhood friends lived in the area, and they are part of the fleeting memory of how we got into graffiti.

Something connects this situation to the walls of the disused railway station building behind grandad's cottage. I recall revisiting those images later and filling a sketchbook with the designs. The gang shared my interest after I showed the symbols. Each evening after that, we would meet at my house and pour over the drawings as though they were our homework.

Soon after, we would meet for adventure. We scrounged an all zone pass and jumped on the underground. Our local station took us to all parts of London, north, south, east, and west. The rail lines ran like spider webs through a dense forest. We stopped at various stations to leave our calling card, first our tags and then our graffiti. Others, more skilled and practiced than we were, had left their marks on the brickwork of embankment walls, tunnels, and viaducts. The large, heavy swaths of color and the personality imparted by the designs fascinated me. Over time, our wayward spraying improved. I must admit, I soon got to be the best amongst us. I came up with my tag, cutting stencils and planning where to best display my work. A multi-colored mushroom cloud hanging over an empty faced grin of a Cheshire cat, 'Bomber' took off.

We carried on until we graduated from school. I spent the first years attending Central Saint Martins at the University of the Arts London, graduating with a diploma in graphic design. A path towards a career with a marketing company glistened on the horizon. Additional study, then a steady career in front of a screen designing logos and letterheads, beckoned.

My guidance advisor, Mrs. Goodyear, even got me interviews at two very well-known design companies. She had contacts. You just wouldn't realize it by the way she dressed. Nothing fashionable or creative about the loose cable knit woolen cardigans that hung from her most times of the year, hot, cold, wet, or dry. I can remember those awful clothes even now, anyone of them would qualify for entry to the local 'ugly sweater' competition. But I understood then a career was not for me. I made a choice to release myself from further study. Another step towards my current situation.

I should have done what she advised, but I just couldn't see myself stuck in an office for eight hours a day, churning out someone else's ideas. When the tea chest opened up its contents, like an oyster spitting out a pearl, an opportunity to follow my path. I had a couple of tattoos done when I was at college and became fascinated with the colors and designs. The level of trust clients had in the artist was immense. These things were permanent. You couldn't wash them off or paint over them like most of my graffiti had been. I want my art to be permanent, so here I am.

6. REASON

Every tattoo carries a reason beneath its ink. As I found almost immediately after setting up my shop, my clients all have a story. A tattoo decorates the wearer, a medal of physical pain, sometimes a concealer of psychological damage, a fashion statement. A flag most likely linked to an event, an acquaintance, hero, some achievement, or a disappointment. They wear the resultant artwork as a talking point to bathe or soothe the story.

The day my life turned upside down, from light to dark. The day, or should I say the twilight evening, that I met her, Lucy. Saturday October the 24th, a day cloaked in the comfort of an English autumn jacket, had started bright, carrying no sign of what was to come.

I didn't get many customers during this time. Even after the lockdown ended back in July, people were still worried about the virus and kept to themselves. I remember the color of the sky, a bright blue, the same shade as the azure ink I used deliberately to make some of my designs pop. It was then that my first customer for months walked in off the street.

"Come on in and take a seat."

In she came, dropping the coat from her hunched shoulders and hanging it on the hook beside the door before following my direction and sinking into the comfort of the work chair. She twitched as I approached. I sat on my stool and readied myself to hear her story.

"Doing OK today?"

"Yeah, best I can be, very apprehensive about the pain."

"I don't want you to be worried about that. You'll feel something, but if it gets too much, we can take a break whenever you need."

"How long will this take? It's just I need to be somewhere at two."

"We have plenty of time." I said, smiling and contacting the deep emotion carried in her eyes.

She sat nervously in the chair, fidgeting back and forth. She was a woman in her mid-thirties. Although she smiled at where the work would go, it wasn't an expression of joy. Her eyes betrayed the hurt hidden beneath. A glassy sadness coating their surface as her mind slipped back to re-imagine her story.

Pulling the fingers of my disposable gloves to get them in place, told her it would be OK. She jumped as the gloves snapped against my flesh. This would be difficult if she couldn't keep still. I shaved and disinfected her right upper arm, the spot to be worked on. She confirmed the design and the colors she wanted to show in the butterfly's wings. It was then she unloaded her story.

I placed the traced design across her arm and marked certain points with an orange sharpie as I listened. The reason for the visit was a sadness, and I looked at her face again. The dark half-moon shadows under her eyes set the backdrop, which informed anyone who cared to look. Trouble is, few did, until a tattoo advertised an openness to discussion. It was common, with only a few exceptions, they would wind the explanation for having work done in my shop around a sadness. I let her spill her hurt while I listened and worked.

I listened to a story about a young autistic girl who folded origami shapes. It was her only way of communicating with her mother, Charlie.

Charlie came to me during her lunch and asked for a small yellow origami butterfly to be drawn on her left arm. As high as possible, above the short sleeve of her tee-shirt.

I hoped that, in instances like hers, the pain experienced while undergoing the work would replace some of the emotional pain carried within the reason for the design. I'm not sure that was the case.

We finished before noon, and she hurried away with a thank you and stifled tears. I closed the shop and walked up the street to the café. A quick sandwich and a hot coffee later, I returned to my studio. The afternoon passed without further business. It was getting late, so I set about tidying up and cleaning the equipment. It was just after 4 p.m.

The deepening late October sky and the folks scurrying by the shop on their way home marked the end of the day. I didn't expect any new business, but it wouldn't be unusual for someone to put their head through the door to enquire about opening hours and costs. The interaction would be brief, usually accompanied by a quick thumb through one of the flash books, my collections of standard stock images.

I was in the back-office area, readying the blue-light autoclave, when I heard the buzzer connected to the door sound as it opened. I shouted through the dividing doorway. "The catalogues are on the side. I'll be with you in a moment."

In reply, a gentle whispering of a young woman's

voice filled the air in greater proportion to the volume it carried.

7. LUCY

The answer came without hesitation, her voice humming between the rooms. "No reason to hurry. I have my request settled, and precise, in mind."

The words carried upon a melody which transported them through distance, being unaffected by obstruction.

"That's good. Maybe we can make you an appointment for later next week. I'll need some time with you to hear your story." I said, walking through the doorway into the inking area, and stopping dead in my tracks. There she was, a demure young woman, in appearance not yet in her twenties. She looked straight at me with those piercing cold blue eyes which pushed and jostled into my inner self. Twisting and scrabbling as they groped like roots of a tree, searching for more in a barren soil. If I knew then that I was more right than wrong, I may have sent her on her way. Or tried at least, but I'm sure there was no other option.

She tilted her head and twisted it in my direction, bouncing the volume of her strawberry blond hair across her brow. The mass undulated as one, as it wrapped down and around both sides of her slim face. Her bright crimson lips arched, unzipping a half smile. I stood frozen in wide-eyed awe. She was beautiful, in a way that struck you without effort. Lost for a moment, my mind was blank.

"Gregory." She said. Not a question, but a statement.

"Yes, But I don't think we have met, have we?"

"Not met, but we do know you. I am here to help."

"Help?"

"Yes, I will tell you more in a moment, but first I need to know. Do you have the practice, the art of the pen?" She asked.

Art of the pen. Why would she phrase it in such a way? The sign was clear, 'Tattooist' it said, on the neon sign over my door.

"Well, if your question is 'do I ink tattoos?' Then yes, I have the art of the pen." I resisted the urge to accompany the answer with air quotes, but thought better of it.

"Then the pen. It draws the art on flesh, marking upon it characters which have a permanence?" She said. Again, her phrasing unusual. An accent held in her voice; she wasn't from around here. It was then I picked up a version of northern English 'Geordie', although it was a non-industrial version.

"Yes, characters and pictures. Anything you need. I have several catalogues of flash designs over there, everything; animals, plants, dragons, fish, logos, whatever you're looking for."

I pointed to the shelf behind her. Four folders, each with at least filled with sixty laminated pages, brimming with examples of designs. I use them as a basis for the end product; to reflect on whatever story the client has to tell.

"Or, if there's nothing in there you like, I can make something from your own ideas. I'm due to close the shop though soon. If you have a thought about what you're looking for, I have open appointments for next week."

But she didn't respond or turn to look. Instead, she held out her hand, palm up.

"The pen, let me see it."

My policy of not allowing clients to handle any of my equipment disappeared without any resistance. Her voice held in the air, a vibrating command, giving me no option other than to follow its demand.

8. THE PEN

I turned and took the pen from its holder, disconnecting the power cable, which ran from the foot operated control pedal beneath my stool. I passed my faithful Cheyenne Hawk rotary tattoo pen into her outstretched hand.

"How does this instrument impart its work?" She said.

Moving to my workbench, I pulled a disposable needle cartridge from the middle draw and removed it from its package. I beckoned for her to return the pen, and she handed it back. I placed the needle into its socket and returned it to her to study. As I lowered the instrument back into her hand, my fingertips brushed her outstretched palm. The skin felt smooth and brittle, and as icy as the stare she gave as I caught her glance.

"Didn't realize it was so cold out there." I said. She didn't respond, instead she examined the tattoo pen. Turning it between her hands and feeling its weight.

"This piece?" She patted the tip on its end.

"The row of small needles carries the ink into the skin. Careful of the points." She wasn't and deliberately stuck her left thumb firmly on the spikes. The needles pierced her flesh, drawing a small dot of blood. She didn't flinch and pushed her thumb to her mouth. She slurped the dot away with a lick of her tongue. A small bead of blood remained on her bottom lip until her tongue snapped it away.

"Hmm. You bless the pen?"

"What do you mean, is it kosher?"

"It has the blessing of the angels?"

I guffawed, blowing out a stifled laugh. "No, I don't have it blessed. I've never heard of anyone having their tattoo pen blessed."

She didn't react other than to stare at me with a bland, quizzical expression. An emotionless, deep gaze.

"Then how is it cleansed?" She said.

"I have a machine. Don't worry." I turned and pointed to the back office. "The blue light of the autoclave sterilizes and removes everything from the pen. The needle is disposable. It's totally clean when it comes out of there."

"No, it requires a fumigation within this hour, the hour of Mercury." I looked at the clock on the wall. It was 4:10 p.m. I didn't know what she meant by 'the hour of Mercury.' I discovered later that the day and night had hours, not the same as we would see on the face of an ordinary clock, but her hours. Occult hours dependent on the movement of the Sun, Moon and five of the planets, Saturn, Jupiter, Mars. Venus and Mercury. Those hours changed as the Earth moved along its track.

"I'm sorry, but I'm closing the shop. I'm done for today. You can make an appointment. I think I have some time on Wednesday."

Before I could say anything more, she continued, clasping the tattoo pen between her palms, and tilting her head backwards towards the ceiling, "Ababaloy, Samoy, Escavor, Adonay. By my measure, I expel all illusion from this instrument, that it may effectively keep within it the virtue necessary for all things which are used in this art, marking upon flesh the characters and conjurations of their calling. Amen."

She lowered her head and opened her hands, setting the pen flat into her left palm. The small finger of her right hand extended. The fingernail shaped as a sharp 'V'. Drawing it across the metal, the nail cut into the body. How, I don't know. The tip of her nail engraving with a high-pitched scratch. When she was done, the marks ran neatly down the side of the instrument, as though they had always been there. A series of Arabic characters they meant nothing to me.

She continued, cupping the pen between her hands, chanting in a deeper frequency which resonated through my bones. "I exorcise thee, creature of Ink, by Anston, Cerreton, Stimulator, Adonay, and by the name of him whose one word created all and can achieve all, that so thou shall assist my officer in his work, that my work accomplishes my will, that this quill drives out all illusions and complications of the physical word. Its body fulfilled with the permission of God, who rules in all things and through all things, everywhere and forever. Amen."

9. ROSE

She handed the pen back to me, turned swiftly to my worktable at her side and tore a sliver of tracing paper from the roll. Flattening the strip, she used the same pointed fingernail to sketch out a design. Having finished it in a flash, she thrust it towards my face. Squinting to focus on the image she had provided gave me no idea what it meant. I had not seen a symbol like it before, a series of scribbles which swam amongst themselves. I would see more like it after this day.

Removing the paper from between us, our eyes met. She stared into me, her voice raised, not in volume but in a vibrating intensity.

"You must mark this character exactly as described with permanence upon the scar of my murder." She commanded.

"Your murder?"

"You cannot hope to believe who I am yet, and what condition brought me here, Gregory

Charles Bentley." She said. A curl of sartorial elegance transformed the corner of her mouth, then dissolved as quickly as it had appeared. My question of her use of murder fell from my mind, replaced with another question. How did she know my name? Only my family, by that I mean my immediate family, knows my full name. Before I could question her more about it, this strange and frightful woman said.

"We must make the mark at the hour of Mars, the midnight of today." She gripped the v-neckline of her dress with both hands and pulled it apart. The opening revealed a circular scar the size of a distorted fist in the center of her chest and over her breastbone.

A rough light brown color, the skin, which had healed over the hole, had melted in place, then reformed. Like a third-degree burn, where the skin runs and forms droplets as it solidifies. I didn't want to, but I stared for longer than I should at the mark as I comprehended what she had said.

"Midnight! I don't think you understand. I'm closing the shop. Maybe you can come in on Monday when I'm open?" I had never tattooed over such a scar, or any scar. I wasn't sure that the leathery skin would receive my ink.

"No, you will do it this day!" She demanded. Her face deformed in an expression of anger, an underlying identity breaking through the illusion of beauty.

"I follow the teachings of the True Grimoire, the most approved keys of Solomon. The sacred incantations of angels, spirits, sorcery, and necromancy. The right to call angels to sit upon our destiny. This information passed to me through my master Mammon's blood and my resurrection. And now you will be my instrument of the calling."

Her eyes turned from blue to red, a burning red. The color carrying the demand with it. I felt myself weaken under their glare. There was nothing I could do to resist. My spirit left me just as I reached within to find it. Paralyzed, I could do nothing but obey her command. Who the hell was she?

10. ANGELS

As if in answer to my silent question, she introduced herself. In a way that I know now only 'She' would.

"In undertaking my work, Gregory Bentley, you are entering an explicit pact with me, and only me, Lucy, through the will of Singambuth. You commit to follow and complete my commands as I instruct."

I could not resist in replying with a croaked, "Yes." My mouth and lips were dry and cracked. It was then that Lucy chanted another of her incantations. She closed her eyes and in a robotic low voice sang.

"Lord God Almighty, He who rules over every creature, reigning through all eternity, he who fulfills great wonders, grant unto us the grace of Thy Holy Spirit through this pen. Bless it, sanctify it and confer upon it a specific virtue, so that whatsoever is said, whatsoever we desire to do and to write herewith, may succeed through Thee, Most Holy Prince Mammon. Amen."

The words made some sense, but I didn't have any idea of the intent of the incantation. I was standing, swaying on my feet. The words hung in my mind like clothes in a wardrobe, resonating, connecting with something primal. As she continued, I steadied myself and without thinking about it, placed a measure of ink ready in my mixing canister.

As soon as she finished, Lucy sat in my client chair, as I called it, with a thud and span it around to face me. I moved towards her with my ink cannister and tattoo pen at the ready. With a wave of her hand, she stopped me, took the container, and threw its contents to the other side of the shop.

Crimson fluid arched across the room until it met the surface of the wall, splattering, then dripping down the wallpaper in a steady stream like wax on a candle. Turning the cup to divest all of its contents, she wiped the insides clean with the hem of her dress. The material showed no mark, but the container was completely empty. She held the now vacant container upright between her knees.

Lucy pulled at the cuff of her left sleeve and poked her long, white fingers inside. A small gauze packet emerged, trapped between her index and middle fingers as she withdrew them. She placed the top of the packet, more like a small sack, between her teeth and gnawed away the string which held it shut around its neck. Lucy spat out the thread as it surrendered its grip; the sack opened.

Then she poured its powdery, yellowy contents into the container. Without hesitation, she pushed the same fingernail that she had used to engrave the scribble onto my pen into her left wrist and turned it back and forth as it pierced the skin. It had more functions than a regular Swiss pocketknife. I observed her face. There was no sign of pain or discomfort, only a look of satisfaction as the nail broke through the flesh.

She withdrew the fingernail, and the volcano of raised skin erupted. A trickle of blood filled the pot as she held the wound above it. The blood poured into the pot, swirling the powder around to dissolve as soon as the fluid made contact. The consistency of the resultant mixture being like that of my inks. She waved her hand above the filled pot and spoke, again singing the words.

"I exorcise you, the body of this Ink, by the names Satanackia and Agalierap and by the name of he who created all by one word, and who can achieve all, so that you shall assist me in my work, and so accomplish this work by my desire, and brought to a successful end through the agreement of He who rules all things, and through all things, omnipresent and eternal. Amen."

Again, the sound the words and the singing voice on which they travelled entered my head and bounded around the space between my ears. It was like being in a concert hall listening to the world's best opera singer. And God knows I hate opera.

11. INK

"This is the pigment you shall use. First to imprint the character as I have drawn and then to design over it the illusion of a flower, a perfect red rose. The design shall cover this scar from the sight of eyes." She said, running the fingertips of both hands around the perimeter of her deformity. "I need to be most beautiful. So beautiful that children may wonder at me, and name me as they have done so before."

I can't recall the wait until midnight. The seven hours seemed to pass in an instant. The clock on the wall didn't lie, did it? One moment it was 4:35 p.m. the next 12:03 a.m. I felt dizzy but strangely awake. The night seemed brighter and Lucy vibrant, if not paler, in complexion. She ordered me to complete the tattoo within the hour. It would normally take me at least three, if not four, hours to complete the design she demanded. But my pen seemed lighter, able to impart the design the moment I thought about my next stroke. My hand remained steady and required no rest for the duration of the work. The petals of the flower filling with shading as the gun moved effortlessly side to side, like the head of a dot matrix printer.

One thing that surprised me was the ease with which the ink flowed and stabilized the skin of the scar. The needles passed easily through the melted and solidified dermis and smoothed the bubbled surface as soon as it absorbed the blood ink. The staccato sound of the rotary motor ceased. I finished by wiping the excess fluid away and stepped backwards to admire my work. It looked like one of the best pieces I had ever done. The rose hid the scar and the script beneath.

Lucy slid out of the chair and, with eyes returned to their original blue color, she poured into my soul and said.

"You have done fine work and will now impart the symbol of the angel Morail upon the forearm of the hand which carries the pen. I shall draw the symbol and you will thereafter be able to call on the power of camouflage." She drew out the symbol on a portion of tracing paper and I obliged by preparing my skin and then engraving the sign on my right forearm. I'm useless with my left hand but found that the pen guided the imprint with little control or direction on my part.

After I marked the symbol, I camouflaged it with a chameleon, the green, red, and yellow shading covering the underlying symbol. Quite fitting, I thought. "Finished." I said. Lucy drew her face close to my work and inspected it. Moving her point of view to follow the outline, scrutinizing each millimeter of the design.

"Perfect." She said, drawing herself upright.

Brushing the area of the mark with the tips of her fingers, Lucy chanted the script, just as she had done so before. The words telling of the pact rolled off her tongue, destined to hang and flutter in the air like drying linen.

12. SEVENTEEN

Lucy's voice jabbed and rippled the center of my chest, like standing in front of a giant bass speaker. My heartbeat strengthened and my body shook and vibrated in time with the words. Lucy gestured with both hands for me to sit in the chair. There was other choice but to comply. I realized how rare it was for me to sit in the client's chair before now; I reserved it for my customers. Anyway, my legs were losing strength, so I motioned towards the chair, hoping to sit before my knees gave way. I just made it, because before I was down, they buckled. I hitched myself backwards into the soft leather with a squirm, just before it was too late, avoiding an end on the floor. She had established a level of control which, no matter how hard I tried, I could never break. I was powerless to resist and slumped in resignation. It was then she told me her story. Well, it was a story.

"Listen to my voice Greg, listen close to my voice. I need to impart this information. It is information connected to the purpose we have for you. You understand we have entered a sacred pact together?"

She stopped and stared into my eye, waiting for a response. I nodded once, and that's all she required before continuing.

"My part of this deal is to deliver to the point of your pen eighteen symbols, each of which you will transfer and camouflage onto a carrier. The carrier will, in return, receive the condition of the angel which they represent. You are the first." She said, walking in a clockwise direction and circling around where I sat. The point of that sharpened fingernail made a scratching sound as it brushed along the leather headrest as she disappeared from my view. She didn't mean 'angel', a term to which I attached meaning.

"My world exists parallel to your own. Filled by beings who influence your reality, a world of superior angels." She said, then continued by reciting the names of the angel spirits in a hushed voice. "Clauneck, Musisin, Bechard, Frimost, Khil, Mersilde, Clisthert, Sirshade, Hicpacth, Humots, Segal, Frucissiere, Guland, Surgat, Morail, Frutimiere, Huictiigaras."

Sinking deeper into the chair, and hypnotized by her words, I tracked her until she moved behind me. Following her a trail of sickly colored sound, flaking and swirling like she was shedding her skin into a washed-out pastel rainbow. Falling into the air as she passed in front, before she circled around again and again.

"Lucifer, Beelzebuth and Astaroth. Thou art my superiors and masters of Mammon and the seventeen, I call upon you to protect our servant Morail. You. Destined to hold the instrument of his command."

Lucifer? I knew of Lucifer, well who doesn't? But the names of the others were new to me. They were going to be brought into contact with this world. She called them 'angels' but I, with my limited knowledge of religious script, knew God and the devil described them differently. Sermons preached every Sunday by Reverend Cornet at St. Joseph's reinforced that opinion. We were regulars at the church until I was around twelve. I don't recall why we stopped going or even the last time I went. Perhaps I wouldn't be in this position and writing this account if I had been more of a regular. Maybe I would have an offer of protection from these demons?

"The shape of each carrier is of no importance. The angels are not themselves of matter or form and will only occupy a body in appearance. A host suitable for their intended manifestation and intent."

My head struggled to take in all what was being said and its consequence. I regained some clarity of mind and asked Lucy. "Why do you use me? Why do you seek to summon them?"

"A promise made and revenge to be taken." She replied, the corners of her lips curled upwards. Only, it wasn't a smile.

13. NIGHTMARE

I half blinked and, with some effort, forced my eyes to open. Their lids were heavy after the sort of sleep, which made it feel like it was too early to wake. The room was bright, filled with the gloss of white sunlight as it poured without restraint through my bedroom window. The brightness splashed onto the wall above my head, pushing me down into the comfort of the blankets now wrapped so tight I couldn't move.

With a groan, I turned to the bedside table. On it was the photo of my family, the five of us, standing on a summer beach at Brighton, hair blown in all directions, the last family holiday. Beside the picture, the green digital display of my alarm clock showed 07:28 a.m. I leant across and hit its button. I had beaten its morning crow for the first time in weeks.

The bells of St. Joseph's church peeled in organized chaos, and through the drawn curtains, silhouettes of pigeons released from their roost in the bell tower danced back and forth like dark snowflakes. There was no recollection of the moment I fell into bed last night, but I remember the dark nightmare swirling before I woke.

With a reluctance often accompanied with a hangover, I eased myself onto my elbows, then hitched into a seated position, pushing my back against the headboard. I let out a long yodeling yawn and ruffled all my fingers through my hair, then dragged their tips down my face. My unshaven jowls stretched, and that's when I noticed it. There, on my right forearm, beside the image of a grinning Cheshire cat, was the new bright ink of a chameleon.

Puzzled, I pulled at the image to dislodge the imprint. It was sore; the mark was new, painful, and permanent. Was the nightmare real? How could it be? My head spun as I questioned my sanity. The events of last night recalled and swirling in my head like pigeons in the sun.

I stretched a tee-shirt over my head; it smoothed my hair. A pair of pants followed. A few steps later, I was down three flights of stairs. I opened the door to the studio, expecting to see the room in disarray and littered with the activity of the night before.

Instead, everything was in its place. The chair was clean and rotated to its regular position, pointing towards the door. Someone had stowed each piece of equipment in its place. I glanced to the wall where, in the dream, 'Lucy' had thrown the ink. I moved across the room, spinning the chair as I passed, and noticed a slight scratch on the headrest as it revolved. She did that in the dream, didn't she?

My eyes tracked to the far wall, to the place where the ink had splattered and stained the wallpaper. I approached closer to the spot to inspect my recollection of the place of impact. I rubbed my left palm across the area. It was smooth, no mark, no stain, no shadow. From the corner of my eye, the green light of the autoclave power button illuminated the darkness of the storeroom. The tattoo pen would be inside, the sterilization program having done its job. I opened the door with a click.

The pen lay on its side in the same place and orientation I would place it. The light caught and flashed across the markings, scratched deep into the metal handle. I paused and shivered, THE markings of Lucy. With some hesitation, I reached inside the machine to remove the pen. The interior ultra-violet blue light of the autoclave illuminated my forearm, together with the area of the new tattoo. A black mound appeared on my arm as the ink of the chameleon lost its color. I looked on in puzzlement as something moved within the deep of the tattoo. Becoming enlivened by the energy of the blue light, a strange mark raised itself out of my flesh. The scarified mark of my 'angel' burst into this dimension.

14. WAIT

It was true then. The meeting. The events and actions of the night before all happened. I shuddered again. Lucy, when would she return? I didn't know so I waited.

Six days passed without a visit. I kept to an unspoken routine, a day-to-day timeline, sleeping, waking, and waiting. A program running my actions. I remained in my apartment; the shop closed to visitors. Even if I wanted to, I knew I couldn't move any further afield. Locked inside by an invisible geo-fenced wall. The internet was my only method of interacting with the outside world, but even then, I sensed I was being monitored. The social network sites always seemed to be down when I attempted to access them. My email would not leave my outbox. Anonymous hands delivered food and other supplies to my door. I waited still, dreaming each night in vivid detail of strange events and different worlds.

Days came and went with no sign of Lucy or her intention. That was, until the night, a week after her first visit. I was sleeping, encased within a subconscious swirling realm. A dark world, figures visited and spoke to me. Featureless faces uttering riddling grunts. Their unformed words made no sense. The darkness turned into a grey mist and the figures dissolved into shadows. Everything went quiet, apart from the whipping and cracking of fallen leaves.

The dream thickened and wove around itself. Edges mixed and formed a loud tornado. Within the shrill of the funnel, mist and debris revolved, tighter and tighter. The mass whistled and morphed into a figure, a familiar form. A crescendo fell silent, then she appeared. It was Lucy, just as I remembered her. Razor blue eyes and tendril like voice spinning my dream into reality. Everything became still as she touched my soul and said.

"I am here, Gregory. Awake, it's time for the first marking."

I awoke with a start. A dim half-moon, which ebbed behind clouds as they scurried across its face illuminated the dark of my room, throwing intermittent shadows across the walls. I stared at the ceiling, knowing I had broken from a dream. A dream, that was all it was, all it could be. I closed my eyes, hoping to avoid a return to the visions that had awoken me. As I drifted back into sleep, a hand gripped my shoulder, shaking me hard three times. I stifled a scream into a "huh" and sat upright. There, at the foot of my bed, the glow of those sharp blue eyes. Lucy stood beside a shadow of another human form.

"Here we are, Gregory, as I foretold. I bring to you, at the hour of Mars, the first of the angels for the ceremony of the art. Ready your pen."

Over the next seven weeks, a steady stream of clients appeared, all accompanied by Lucy. The visits timed to occur within the hour of Mars whenever that would be, day or night. I imprinted the characters using Lucy's blood ink, with the knowledge they would become energized to channel the angels which they represented. Eighteen if you include me.

The fifth or sixth client, I would still call them clients, but these people were more like wax-work figures, was my old childhood friend Winston. He was a tall man, taller than I recalled, about six-four. His dark skin carried a listless, slimy texture. I notice skin; it being the contact point of my interaction. An awareness its condition provides a window into my client's life. I suppose in the same way a dentist observes a person's teeth when they first meet.

The last I had heard of Winston was he that he was working in his family's construction business, Cheriton Builders. He always looked confident. Now he looked dazed and vacant, just like all the others. When I think of it, none of them displayed any spark of individual consciousness. They all hung onto Lucy's command. Was I of the same appearance and manner? Winston's only words, as were all the others, were the chanted incantation which preceded the designated mark being applied.

As they came to my shop to receive the symbol, Lucy would announce their controlling angel and the particular power of influence. She would then provide me with what she called a 'parchment' of the symbol to be tattooed. A scrap of felt like paper. My task, as noted by my mark and the power it dispersed, is to camouflage the symbol with an overlay which wouldn't raise too much notice.

After every imprint, Lucy would take the parchment from my possession and destroy it. The material rolled into a ball and then burning in her palm. The flame would flare in a different color each time. Lucy would then press her tongue into the ashes and consume them in entirety, licking her palm clean.

Other than my memory, there was no record of the design. No one will identify who bares the mark, and what power they imbued. What she didn't count on was my ability to remember any tattoo I draw. I can recount any sketch or artwork that I've ever done. A sort of photographic memory, I suppose. They are all a part of me and not forgotten. It is this ability which allows me to reconstruct the symbols within this journal. It is also the case that during this time, I had no other work to cloud my mind. Lucy had ensured that none of my regular clients would return. How and what she had done to achieve the feat I dare not consider.

From observation, I know the names of the angels which the marks represent. Together with an idea of the recipient's profession, they would continue in their human business until they were called. Lucy did not inform me of these facts, but I became determined to record as much as I could as soon after the visits as possible. Then I tied the words of Lucy with what I recalled through the clothing and appearance of the supposed angel. I came to the assumptions you find attached.

My symbol relates to Morail. I think you agree this makes sense. The angel who has power over camouflage, and that's what she has conscripted me for. I disguise the marks with covering tattoos, which no one would pick as being out of the ordinary. Apart from the individual bearers, only I and Lucy know the complete picture. I think that alone places me in a vulnerable position. I know too much, which is why I'm recording this account and counting down the seventeen.

15. END

You may find it strange perhaps, after reading this account, to imagine without hesitation that all of it is true. Even as I flounder within the isolation, I too have the same question. My love is to do what I do. It's a fact though that the enjoyment has waned from my interactions with 'Her'. After all, it's my calling, something I can do without effort. Sketch and draw and tell stories through my art.

Today I opened up my laptop, it booted, and I clicked to open Google. The screen brightened as it spang into life. The ubiquitous 'Google Doodle' occupied the center of the screen. I ran the pointer into the empty white box and typed astrological hour calculator.

I stopped for a moment. Right now, it seemed to be an error on Lucy's part not to restrict my access to the internet. She had controlled my ability to leave the confines of my workplace. Maybe she wasn't aware or concerned about the power at the tip of my fingers, or just maybe she did not comprehend that it existed.

A blink and the top ten search results filled the screen. I clicked on the first, which led to the corresponding Wikipedia page. I had noted the similarity wrapped into the randomness of the hour she brought her subjects to the shop. Each session would begin with Lucy mentioning the hour of Mars. It must be that there is a parallel clock to the one which we all use. The second hands being the only consistency between the two. The alternative, the one that sits behind our reality. I read the page as it opened, scrolling as I felt the rush of knowledge and satisfaction as the words confirmed my theory.

The Babylonians had set out this measurement many hundreds of years ago, dating before the birth of Christ. I gorged on the information, a full descriptive of the system, and its observance of the seven classical planets. I returned to the search results and clicked on another site which offered a live astronomical hour calculator. Lunarium.co.uk.

My scribbled note of all the previous visits by Lucy and her cohorts lay crumpled beside the keyboard. I correlated a search of past and future divisions of the day with my records. I entered the time of each session. The results confirmed the hours that the marks had to be written into the skin. The next scheduled hour would arrive in ten minutes. If this was the schedule, then Lucy would bring the bearer of the remaining symbol, the seventeenth, today.

It still mystified me how Lucy arrived at my shop, gaining access without alarm. No vehicle, Uber, taxi, or bus brought her to my door. There was never any warning of her approach. I sat on the edge of my bed, knowing that I had a maximum of thirty minutes until the hour of Mars to get out. She or one of her followers could watch the main entrance. I didn't want that to be as far as I got. The back door was an alternative, but it exited to the rear yard and then onto an alley which led onto the street beside my store front.

From my bedroom window, I gazed down onto the back yards below. My breath clouded the cold pane, and I rubbed the glass with the side of my hand to clear away the fog. The slate of the pitched roof was the same color as the clouds which filled the sky. A sign of coming snow. Maybe I could get onto the roof and from there lower myself onto the external stairway behind Boyles, the end building of the row. The stairway led into a yard and to the rear entrance of the funeral home.

Then, from below, I hear the shop door open and her call. Lucy was delivering the last client. The final bearer of the sacred marking. The sign of Huictiigaras, which I will not get to know, if I escape. After I apply this symbol, would I become surplus to her needs? There would be no further reason for my work. I'm not hanging around to find out. I need to escape, I always have, but for whatever reason, I've not been able to process that until now.

The snow was falling, making the roof a treacherous obstacle, but one I would need to navigate. Lucy was getting impatient and closer. The stairs creaked as she approached, getting closer and closer.

"Gregory, I am here for your service. Come to me now." She called. The grip of the tendrils of her voice wrapped themselves around my throat. The handle of the locked door to my bedroom rattled. There's something I remember, but I've no time to think. No time to waste.

I'm not answering. My escape is across the roof to the stairway and down to safety. If all goes as planned, then we will read this account together. If not, then I hope these words will help you stop Lucy and her followers unleashing their plan upon this city. I can hear her footsteps travelling with a steady stomp up the stairway. I shall hide this journal and go, we shall meet, I know it.

16. THE SEALS

Clauneck – Stock Trader/Financial

Musisin – Politian?

Bechaud – Meteriologist

Frimost - Actor

Klepoth – Nurse

Khil - Builder

Mersilde - Driver

Clisthert – Electrician

Sirchade – Car salesman

Segal - photographer

Hicpacth – Computer expert/Hacker

Humots – Teacher/Librarian

Frucissiere – Mortician

*Guland – Scientist/
biologist/chemist*

Surgat - Locksmith

*Morail – The marker
– my symbol*

Frutimiere – Chef/cook

Huictiigaras - Unknown

A. LUCY RISING

I t was the day when autumn stilled its colorful momentum. The golden and radiant oranges of dying foliage turning into the muddy dark browns expected of the coming winter. A cooling but stiffening breeze blew through the treetops, twisting leaves away from their tenuous grip. Branches and stems rattled like maracas, their discarded cargo sent tumbling earthwards. As the leaves fell, a microscopic drizzle applied a weighty coating to their surface.

Beneath and between the trees, a meandering path, its route avoiding an unorganized arrangement of stones and statues. On it, the figures of two men strode with purpose. Cherry was the taller of the two. He walked half a pace ahead of Brad. By comparison, he was a heavier and wider specimen. Brad gripped his woolen cap with both hands, holding it against his balding head in fear of the gusts. The men's heavy work boots squashing the leaves into a slimy, slippery wafer underfoot. Cherry stopped, his feet skidding on the hard, slippery ground beneath. He thrust his left arm into Brad's chest. This was what he was looking for.

"There he is, look, Karl Marx."

His grubby fist reached out, filled with a half-eaten roast beef sandwich, and extended a single finger. It waved in the general direction of the oversized bronze head perched atop a tall gray marble plinth. The tomb of Karl Marx, and its unmissable edifice, sat in the eastern section of the Highgate cemetery in London. To Cherry, a hero of sorts. His finger wiggled, the red diamond tattooed on its knuckle wrinkled as the digit continued to motion. The two construction workers stood side by side in awkward consideration of the monument.

Brad adjusted his glasses and squinted his left eye to a tight slit as he spoke, reading aloud the inlaid gold inscription on the front of the grave.

"Workers of all lands untie."

Cherry choked and spat out a chunk of sandwich, thrusting his free hand sideways, and punching Brad hard in his midriff. Not expecting the strike, Brad stumbled. His feet struggled for traction as he performed a jittery dance on the slippery mash of oak leaves beneath his feet. Some sort of Irish jig. While his hands remained planted on his cap.

"Unite. Workers unite! Not Untie! Ya daft nonce."

Cherry chewed twice, and gulped, then took another bite of the sandwich, a breath away from the knuckle.

"It's me dyslexia. And the drizzle." Said Brad. Shifting his weight from one foot to the other with a sliding motion as the leaves gave way beneath the thick soles of his work boots.

"More like your glasses, look at the state of 'em. All marked up and scratched. Blimey, I'm surprised ya can see anything through 'em. You driving the dozer an all."

"Come on, he's dead and buried, just like he should be. Don't know what all the fuss is about. If you want people to visit, make a theme park, not a coffee shop." Brad turned and headed down the path. He continued, muttering as he walked. "Anyway, we better get on. Brookes will be on our backs if we don't get down there pronto."

"Just make sure you can see where I am when you're running that thing. It's a worry. I don't want to end up in here." Cherry shouted after him.

Brad smirked and huffed. They both smiled.

In silence, the two continued along the pathway towards the western section of the graveyard, an area of unorganized gravestones. Cherry finished the slab of white bread by stuffing the crust into his mouth like a hamster as he trailed behind.

The path led them to an area taped off with yellow construction ribbon, which blew and rattled in the wind. The rectangle it formed was just too neat. A sterile area, tied between measured wooden stakes. The perimeter encapsulated a thicket of trees and dense shrubs, old gravestones and tombs sat around its edge. It was strange, as it was the only unused area within the whole site.

The drizzle wafted around the wispy branches and curls of ivy, taking a few of the autumn leaves with it as the breeze continued to ease them from the branches as they bent back and forth.

"Steady on. Here he is."

"Not Karl Marx, is it, eh?" Said Brad as he punched Cherry's arm, then adjusted his glasses by pushing them onto the bridge of his nose with a single finger. They both smiled.

"Now you say it, he looks very much like…"

The two looked towards the man as he approached. A pendulum of swinging arms above a purposeful stride made quick work of the distance between them. The round face, full beard and leathery skin hardened by years of building site supervision showed little in emotion, other than a determination to get things done.

"Alright, you two. Lunch is over. This is the spot. We need the whole thing cleared away and the ground taking down a couple of feet."

The area was the location chosen for a new welcome center for visitors to the cemetery. Somewhere they could learn about the history of the place and all those buried within its grounds while grabbing a hot cup of tea or coffee and a sandwich. Not quite the theme park Brad had recommended.

The man hitched up his sleeve and looked at his wrist. The white Apple watch seemed out of place with the shabby waterproof cuff that covered it.

"It's just gone one, I think." He tapped on the watch's face. "Strange, no signal. I'll be back in a few hours. You should have most of it completed by then."

"Yes, Mr. Brookes. We'll be right on it. Brad is a wizard on the dozer. He is."

"Don't need a wizard. I need it done." Brookes stared at them both before looking again at his watch, murmuring to himself again "no signal", then turned to depart the way he came. "I'll be in the construction office if you need me." He called over his shoulder. At the same moment, the breeze picked up a swirl of leaves, like a mini tornado, which revolved around his words as he strode away.

Grunting, Brad climbed up the side of the excavator,

or 'dozer' as Cherry liked to call it, jumped in the cab, started the engine, and rubbed his knees. A plume of black diesel smoke coughed, then burst from the exhaust as the machine grumbled into life. Cherry took several steps backwards. He didn't trust Brad enough to be in swinging distance of the arm and its jaws. The machine lurched forwards on its tracks for a few yards, stopped dead, then thrust its gaping claw into the mass of trees and shrubs in front of them. Cracking and snapping preempted the vegetation being torn from its home, then without ceremony dumped as crushed and broken remains in a neat pile to the side of the excavator. Brad's hands worked fast at the controls. Brain and machine became one.

After over four hours and three times as many grabs of the claw, the arm disappeared, this time closer into the center of the thicket. Without warning, Cherry squirmed, his hands over his ears as a shuddering scraping echoed around him. The machine jerked as it hit something solid, the sound of metal on stone. Cherry looked towards the cab and Brad. He had already taken his hands off the controls, raising them above his head as an act of surrender.

"Blimey, what have you hit?"

The machine became motionless. Around them, everything fell silent. Brad scrambled from the cab and jumped down beside Cherry. They both stood there for a moment like statues. Brad adjusted his glasses.

"Didn't see a thing."

"You surprise me. We'd better have a look. Let's find out what you've broken this time." Cherry said, turning to Brad, who had lost what little color he had in his face. The blood had drained to his boots. "Come on."

The pair scrambled through the undergrowth, pushing broken branches and tree limbs to either side as they crept into the center of the thicket. The breeze calmed as Cherry stumbled on a stone slab. Deep scores marked where the claw of the excavator had gouged into the moss and root covered surface and ripped it from where it had hidden the doorway to the underground tomb, which it had once sealed.

"Whoa, it's a tomb. Pass the light." Said Cherry.

"How long do you think that's been there?"

"A long time. There's a date there; 1894."

Brad flashed the torch he always carried in his pocket against the stone and its inscription. He handed it to Cherry like a baton in a relay race, "There could be some-one inside." His voice quivered.

"Not scared, are you?"

Brad remained silent, pushing his glasses to the highest part of his nose to look on as Cherry held the torch before him, then disappeared step by step into the tomb. A few seconds passed.

"Brad, come down here. Look at this."

After hesitating for longer than he should have, Brad poked his head through the opening and, with deliberation, stepped down onto the last step. He saw the remains, the feet, the legs, the broken rib cage. A bleached skeletal structure of a body. But there was something wrong with what he saw. Something missing.

"There's no head!" he squealed.

The beam illuminated and then scanned the length of the slab and the remains laying on it, continuing around the chamber until it struck a skull on the floor, like a gleaming pearl.

"There it is! Pass it over." Cherry said, gesticulating in the general direction of the missing piece.

"I'm not touching anything, especially that!" Brad stepped back towards the entrance.

"Come on. You must have knocked it off when the cover came off this place. We don't want to be blamed for disturbing a body, do we? Pass it to me, then we'll call Brookes."

Brad needed little as an invitation. He wanted out of this place as soon as possible. He picked up the skull using the tips of his fingers and held it out in front of him as far as he could before Cherry took hold of it and positioned it in its rightful place.

Brad pulled his cellphone out of his pocket as he climbed out of the chamber. "No signal, Cherry."

"You'll just have to go get him, then."

"Leave you with it." Brad said, as he scurried out of the thicket and back onto the path in search of Brookes.

It was a good hour or more before Brad returned to the excavation area with Brookes in tow. It was just coming up to 6:30 p.m. Behind the clouds; the sun had dipped below the tops of the trees, painting the sky a darkening gray, purple haze as night approached.

"It's in there. Cherry must still be inside.'

Brookes followed the trail to the tomb, brushing aside the remnants of broken branches and their remaining leaves, then disappeared inside. He emerged in a matter of seconds.

"Ok, nice one. You got me there. A graveyard at dusk. So, where is he? No time for practical jokes, Brad. We need to get this cleared away by the end of tomorrow. You pair are behind schedule."

"He's in there, with the body. He must be."

"There's nothing in there. No remains and no Cherry."

B. MURDER

Wednesday morning is the complete opposite of the day before. The cloud and drizzle of the previous evening had given way to a bright late autumn dawn and, for those who took time to notice, the rising sun warmed their faces as they rushed about their business. Detective Sergeant 'Kane' awoke with the same sun issuing thin splinters of light across his face, only moments before the wake-up alarm sounded. He gave a couple of coughs, grunted, threw off his bedsheets, and tottered to the bathroom. After showering, he shaved and slapped his jowls with lotion. His usual breakfast followed, a bowl of muesli watered with the slightest dose of almond milk.

He finished dressing, grabbed his keys from the hook he always stored them on, and marched to his car. A second breakfast with his gaffer, Detective Inspector Charlie Birch. No doubt she would be knee deep in some unhealthy fried meats and such.

Kane arrived close to the meetup twenty minutes

later. He strode through the park off Tanner Street in Bermondsey, South London. A small urban green area with a few tennis courts and a grassy area where dogs could run around under the care of their owners. This early there we no takers for the tennis courts.

A jogger, a young woman dressed in a tracksuit, came bounding along the path towards him, her earbuds drowning out all activity of the world around her. In front of her, a panting bull mastiff, who knew the route much better than his owner. Behind her, a whipping ponytail of braided hair. They came barreling towards the inattentive Kane, the jogger oblivious, as the dog determined the path.

At the last moment, Kane noticed their arrival and danced a trot as he sidestepped backwards, attempting, with a couple of quick steps, to allow the pair to pass. Dancing with the stars, it was not. The raised edge of the path welcomed his foot into a muddy puddle, the thick liquid splattering over his polished boot and onto the razor-sharp hem of his pressed trousers.

"Damn it!!"

He felt the sludge raise above the rim of his heel and the cold soup slither down into his shoe. The best feeling ever, he thought.

"That'll be a thank you then!" He shouted after the

young woman and her dog as they passed.

He shook his foot to remove as much of the mud as he could and cast a sharp glance towards the offenders. The dog turned without missing a stride, its tongue flapping through the side of its mouth as it returned his glance with utter disdain, before continuing on its way.

Kane thrust his right hand into his pressed trouser pocket and removed a bleached white handkerchief. He flapped it in the breeze and its brightness caught the sun. It opened like a parachute, highlighting the monogrammed gold thread of H.G. on its corner. He tipped sideways, losing his balance. His left hand grabbed the trunk of a nearby tree to steady himself and there he stood, like a flamingo on one leg, as he drew up his boot to wipe it down. He remembered his father's words as they rang beyond his ears, "the sign of a man's soul is through the shine of his heals." The white cotton of his handkerchief and its gold monogram turned a dark brown as they soaked up the liquid of the autumn sludge. Freezing in place while he studied the mess, Kane huffed and then reanimated as he continued towards the park gates and the exit onto Bermondsey Street.

Still holding the now filthy cloth between his fingertips, Kane rolled it into a ball. He stepped out of the park onto Bermondsey Street and turned right towards Big Al's café, the meeting place. As he passed a waste bin, he disposed of the handkerchief, throwing it into the small opening of the container with an accuracy which any professional basketball player would have been proud of. He smirked to himself and looked around. The smirk dissolved. He pursed his lips, disappointed no-one had seen the shot.

Bermondsey Street was a bustle of morning commuters and blown leaves. Big Al's café, a typical 'greasy spoon', was somewhere workers of every genre would call in for breakfast. It didn't matter who you were or what you did, especially after a hard night on the town. Kane entered the café, a bell attached to the top of the door give a single chime. As it announced his arrival. No one cared.

"You look rough, mate." He called out to a solitary figure, slumped over a full English breakfast and a steaming mug of tea at the table closest to the window.

"Than usual?" Replied Birch. Her slight frame belied the amount of food she could consume. She recognized the voice and without diverting her attention, commented back.

"Hmm, now you mention it. I might, perhaps for a Wednesday."

He took a chair opposite to her and pushed the plate and place setting away while waving at the small man behind the counter that he needed nothing.

"Always wondered."

"About what?"

"Whether he's 'Big Al' or what?"

Birch sighed and gave him a roll of her eyes. "His name tag says Bob, so it's unlikely, don't you think?"

"Hmm... That answers that, then. Thank you, Sherlock."

"Anyway, I'll be better for this." Charlie picks up one of the two plump sausages on her plate, dips it in a pile of ketchup, then holding it between thumb and index finger waves the glistening length of pork back and forward, pointing it with menace at Kane's face, a moment before reversing its direction and plunging it into her mouth, withdrawing it for a second before taking a large bite. Teeth chomping together with a snap. She waives the remnant back and forth with no care and issues a rasping burp. Kane is the only one in the cafe to react, or for that matter, even notice.

"Jeez, your eating habits don't get any better, do they? You doing that to wind me up?"

"A bit of grease never did for anyone."

"That's what your doctor says, then?"

"I'm alright, he's a right quack."

Purse vibrates.

"I think that's you."

Purse vibrates again and Birch slaps the half-chewed sausage onto her plate with a smash as the entire tabletop rattles. The cafe quiets, just for a tick of the wall clock hanging behind the counter before the hum of conversation and eating recommences.

"Hold on." She fumbles around her case, pulling random items onto the table before retrieving her cell phone and taking the call.

"Birch."

"Yeah, where?"

She points at Kane and makes a gesture like holding a wand with her re-acquired sausage, alerting him to be ready to write the address.

"Highgate Road, the tattooists near St. Joseph's. Yeah, I know that place. What's the story?"

Birch continues to chew as she listens, providing additional fuel to her already overloaded mouth.

"Got it. We'll be there in thirty. You know the drill. Scenes of crimes there? OK."

Birch stuffs her mouth again before she throws her phone back into her bag, followed by all the items she removed as she scrapes them off the tabletop. Kane sits back in his chair and shakes his head, his hair tossing against his forehead. Birch issues another burp. This time it's silent as it pushes out her cheeks and bursts through her pursed lips.

"Got any then? He says.

"What?"

"Tattoos?"

"Yeah, a nice little angel on my arse, amongst others."

"I'd like to see that."

"Sorry, not my type, mate. Anyway, where's your car? We gotta go."

"Two minutes away, Tanner Street, close to the park entrance. And don't forget your sausage."

Birch grins. Kane picks up a napkin and wipes the remnants of mud from his hands. Birch grabs at the remaining sausage, using her fingers like a pair of chopsticks. She swipes with the link at a mountain of ketchup sitting like a dormant volcano on the side of her plate, before stuffing it whole into her mouth. Then, without care, she pinches the synthetic material of her jacket at her waist and cleans the grease from her fingertips, leaving another polka dot to match the others in its vicinity.

"You'll ruin that jacket." Kane says. Birch shrugs, her cheeks bulging with the weight of their contents. The entrance bell chimes above their heads as they leave the café.

On the street, Kane tosses the rolled napkin at the same waste bin. He misses. The napkin unfolds as it falls into the roadway. He scurries to pick it up and pushes it through the slot. This time there were witnesses. Kane shakes his head and strides to Birch's side.

"What's it about then?" He says.

"A murder, by the sound of it. Sliced up and peeled good and proper."

BOOKS BY THIS AUTHOR

Sherlock And Dracula

Seven years after Dracula's apparent demise at the hands of Jonathan Harker and his five compatriots in the forests of the Carpathian Mountains, Sherlock Holmes is asked by Mina Harker to help track down what she believes is the returning vampire before he takes his revenge.

But she may be too late. Can Sherlock and Dr. Watson find the lair of Dracula somewhere in Victorian London before vengeance is served?

www.sherlockdracula.com for more information, maps, evidence, and journals.

Based on the characters Sir Arthur Conan Doyle developed in his works depicting the Adventures of Sherlock Holmes and characters created by Bram Stoker in Dracula.

Whitby Rock

As dawn breaks, a church bell calls for attention in a rural English village. An unidentified body hangs upside down in its belfry. Beneath the swinging corpse are small, individually wrapped candies marked 'Whitby Rock.' It is not long before the case doubles its mystery. Detective Inspector Mary Hunter, a rising star in the police force, sets out to investigate the reason behind the murder and unravel the strands that connect it all. In the middle of it all, Jack Headland, struggling to break free and put his working-class upbringing behind him, becomes entangled with an enigmatic criminal mastermind who tells a mysterious story of contraband, drugs, money laundering, disappearance, and robbery. A link that connects unplanned events in wartime Sweden to a strange hotel on the English coast,

Frankenstein 2035

It's 2035. Beta, a young Austrian scientist, seeks a cure for her only remaining family member, her disabled brother. She understands this is his only hope. After being handed an old recipe for creating life, she accepts an invitation from a mysterious group to join other researchers at an arctic station in Nunavut, Canada. Meanwhile, in that location, divers pull something, preserved by the almost freezing water, from a wreck that has lain at the bottom of the arctic ocean for more than 200 years.

At the station, the team reveals their specialties and finds themselves connected in an experiment to restore the spirit of a man who has been dead for two centuries. Unfortunately, the investigation soon spins out of control, and a horrific sequence of events and personal discoveries erupt within the isolated research station. There is no escape amidst the fury of a freezing arctic storm.

How are the recently discovered elements of quantum mechanics, geomagnetic fields, fractal patterns, and dark matter connected to galvanism and the human spirit? What are the motives of each team? Who is the organization? What links Beta to this mysterious group? Can anyone escape the fury of the arctic and its ancient spirits?

www.ingramcontent.com/pod-product-compliance
Lightning Source LLC
Chambersburg PA
CBHW020543130626
46552CB00007B/2734